ASK THE
CONSTITUTION

Is Every American Adult Allowed to Vote?

Alex Acks

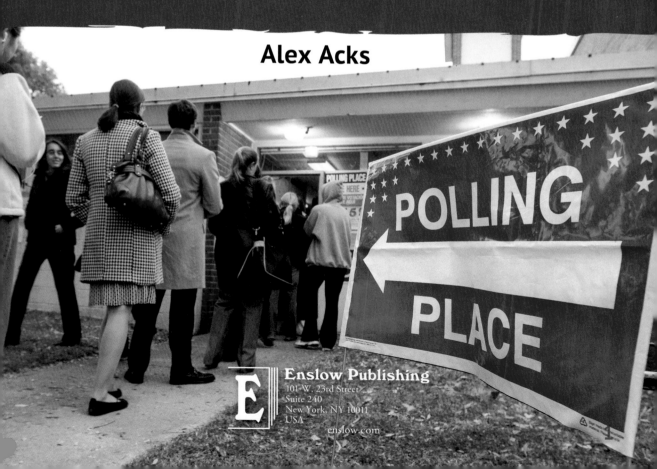

E | **Enslow Publishing**
101 W. 23rd Street
Suite 240
New York, NY 10011
USA

enslow.com

Published in 2020 by Enslow Publishing, LLC
101 W. 23rd Street, Suite 240, New York, NY 10011

Cataloging-in-Publication Data

Names: Acks, Alex.
Title: Is Every American Adult Allowed to Vote? / Alex Acks.
Description: New York : Enslow Publishing, 2020. | Series: Ask the Constitution | Includes bibliographical references and index. | Audience: Grades 5-8.
Identifiers: ISBN 9781978507081 (library bound) | ISBN 9781978508477 (pbk.)
Subjects: LCSH: Suffrage—United States—History—Juvenile literature. | Voting—United States—History—Juvenile literature. | United States. Voting Rights Act of 1965—Juvenile literature.
Classification: LCC JK1846.A299 2020 | DDC 324.6/20973—dc23

Printed in the United States of America

To Our Readers: We have done our best to make sure all website addresses in this book were active and appropriate when we went to press. However, the author and the publisher have no control over and assume no liability for the material available on those websites or on any websites they may link to. Any comments or suggestions can be sent by email to customerservice@enslow.com.

Photo Credits: Cover and p. 1 top, interior pages background (Constitution) Jack R Perry Photography/Shutterstock.com, cover, p. 1 (line of voters) Rob Crandall/Shutterstock.com; p. 7 Margoe Edwards/Shutterstock.com; pp. 9, 14 MPI Archive Photos/Getty Images; p. 10 Lebrecht History/Bridgeman Images; p. 13 © iStockphoto.com/SochAnam; pp. 17, 19 Library of Congress Prints and Photographs Division; p. 20 Everett Historical/Shutterstock.com; p. 22 Hulton Archive/Archive Photos/Getty Images; p. 25 Interim Archives/Archive Photos/Getty Images; p. 27 Bettmann/Getty Images; p. 29 © AP Images; p. 31 blvdone/Shutterstock.com; p. 32 Scott Olson/ Getty Images; p. 35 Portland Press Herald/Getty Images; cover, interior pages (paper scroll) Andrey_Kuzmin/Shutterstock.com.

Contents

Introduction

In August of 2018, some residents of Harris County, Texas, got strange letters in the mail. The letters warned that there was a problem with their voter registration and said if they didn't get information back to the voter registrar within thirty days, their ability to vote would be cancelled.[1] These letters may have broken federal law even as they upset the voters that received them. Federal law says that voter lists should not be changed except under special circumstances within ninety days of an election. The letters were sent after the ninety-day limit had passed.

Ann Harris Bennet, the registrar for Harris County, said she was forced to send the letters by Alan Vera, who filed a formal challenge on the status of four thousand voters in Harris County. Ann Harris Bennet is a member of the Democratic Party, and Alan Vera is a member of the Republican Party. At least fifteen states allow voter registrations to be challenged in ways like Alan Vera did it in Texas. At least twenty states allow voters to be challenged in person when they have gone to a polling place to vote.[2] The Brennan Center for Justice conducted a study that found these laws that allow voter registration to be challenged tend to be used against nonwhite voters most often.[3]

Harris County has the biggest population of any county in Texas—it includes the city of Houston. It is the third most populous county in the United States[4] and the most racially diverse.[5] Texas is a big state with a large influence on the federal government of the United States. With thirty-six representatives in Congress as of the 2010 census, it's second only to California, which has fifty-three.[6] National elections aren't the only ones that matter, however. Like every other voter in America, voters in Texas decide who will make laws in their own state and ordinances in their cities.

This isn't the first time Texas has gotten in trouble with the federal government over how it handles voting. As recently as April of 2018, a federal judge ruled that Texas was breaking the law by not letting people register to vote when they renew or get new drivers licenses.[7] In 2017, courts ruled that a Voter ID law was discriminatory and that Texas's election laws would have to be overseen by the United States Department of Justice.[8] Before the Supreme Court case *Shelby County v. Holder*, Texas was one of nine states required by the Voting Rights Act of 1965 to receive preclearance from the federal government on its voting laws because of its history of discrimination against minority voters.[9]

On the surface, it looks like every adult in America over the age of eighteen can vote. But once someone is registered to vote, that's not the final word. Sometimes an unexpected letter comes in the mail, or worse. The question of who can vote has had a lot of different answers since the Constitution was written—and the answers are still changing today.

1

Voting Rights at the Founding of the United States

Elections, in which the people who are allowed to vote choose between at least two options, have been around for thousands of years. Records show that in ancient Greece, male citizens could vote in decisions that affected the cities they lived in.[1] Elections as we know them today, where officials are elected to represent people, came into being in Europe and America in the 1600s.[2] The British Parliament with its elected House of Commons was familiar to the men who created the Constitution.

But what does the Constitution say about who is allowed to vote?

Voting at the Dawn of America

Before the Constitution of the United States of America created the government that we have today, there was another, very short-lived governing document: The Articles of Confederation. The Articles of Confederation were created because the states—and the men they sent to the Continental Congress—had a lot of reasons to be fearful of a strong central government like the one they were rebelling against in England.[3]

Voting is one of the most direct ways to change the direction of a country; whom you elect impacts all facets of your life, from your health to the environment.

When the Articles of Confederation were created, the new government of the United States was given barely enough power to conduct the Revolutionary War.[4] That lack of power caused the Articles of Confederation to fail and made the creation of the Constitution necessary.[5] The Constitution made the central government bigger and gave it more power.[6]

Under the Articles of Confederation, each state had at least two delegates in the Congress, though each state only got one vote. The delegates were elected by state legislatures,[7] and the administration of these elections was left to the states.[8] When it came time to decide how voting would work in the new Constitution, the choice wasn't simple. There was fierce debate over whether people should be allowed to vote for members of Congress. Roger Sherman of Connecticut didn't want direct voting at all. He said, "The people should have as little to do as may be about the government. They lack information and are constantly liable to be misled."[9]

Others believed in direct democracy. James Madison felt voting was important but saw potential problems with who was allowed to vote. He said in a speech: "The right of suffrage is a fundamental Article in Republican Constitutions. The regulation of it is, at the same time, a task of peculiar delicacy. Allow the right exclusively to property, and the rights of persons may be oppressed... Extend it equally to all, and the rights of property or the claims of justice may be overruled by a majority without property, or interested in measures of injustice."[10]

In the end, the writers of the Constitution decided to take the same path as the Articles of Confederation and left the matter of voting and elections to the states—except they reserved the right for Congress to make laws about it in the future:[11] "The times, places and manner of holding elections for Senators and Representatives, shall be prescribed in each state by the legislature thereof; but the Congress may at any time by law make or alter such regulations."[12]

Religious Tests

Article VI of the Constitution says that, "no religious Test shall ever be required as a Qualification to any Office of public Trust under the United states." This means that the federal government could not require someone to be a particular religion to hold an office or work for the government. But religious tests did exist for voting. Before the Constitution was ratified, several of the colonies excluded Jewish or Catholic people from voting.[13] By 1790, all of those laws had been eliminated, but that happened after the first presidential election of 1789.

ARTICLES

OF

Confederation

AND

Perpetual Union

BETWEEN THE STATES

OF

NEW-HAMPSHIRE, MASSACHUSETTS-BAY, RHODE-ISLAND AND PROVIDENCE PLANTATIONS, CONNECTICUT, NEW-YORK, NEW-JERSEY, PENNSYLVANIA, DELAWARE, MARYLAND, VIRGINIA, NORTH-CAROLINA, SOUTH-CAROLINA AND GEORGIA.

LANCASTER:
PRINTED BY FRANCIS BAILEY.
M,DCC,LXXVII.

The Articles of Confederation was a short-lived document that attempted to do what the Constitution does today. It was a place to begin.

Who Could Vote Under the New Constitution?

In general, after the Constitution went into effect, voting was limited to white men over the age of twenty-one who were Protestants and owned a minimum amount of property. That was only about six percent of the population.[14] However, since the matter was left to the states, there were exceptions to the rule. Some states specifically allowed veterans of the Revolutionary War to vote, even if they didn't own property.

Unmarried and widowed women were allowed to vote in several of the colonies at the founding. Women were still voting in New York, New Hampshire, and Massachusetts during the Articles of Confederation years, but the right was taken away from them by changing state laws before the Constitution. The New Jersey state constitution originally didn't specify the gender of who could vote, as long as they had enough property, so a few women were able to vote.

George Washington was elected the first president of the United States, in 1789. He won all sixty-nine electoral votes and did it again in 1792. These are the only unanimous electoral college wins in history.

In 1790, state law was changed to acknowledge that women could vote. Then seventeen years later, the state changed its laws again and women lost their right to vote in New Jersey.[15,16]

New Jersey also allowed free black men and women who owned property to vote during that time, until the state constitution was changed to restrict voting to only white men.[17] Black men in Pennsylvania were allowed to vote until 1838.[18] Other states that had allowed black people and white women to vote took away that right over time.

Because the right to vote was left to the states and not defined in the Constitution, it could be given or taken away by the whims of the state.

2

Voting Rights for (Almost) All Men

By 1856, the states had abolished all legal barriers to white men voting. North Carolina was the last state to require that voters owned property.[1] But there were many people living under the United States government that still weren't allowed to vote: Native Americans, black people (the majority of whom were still enslaved), and white women.

From almost the beginning of the country, these excluded people and those who believed in equality for all, such as the Quakers,[2] fought to expand the right to vote. State laws could be changed to give or take away voting rights, and only for the people who lived in that state. The best and most lasting way to guarantee the right to vote was to amend the United States Constitution.

The Thirteenth Amendment

On November 9, 1860, South Carolina became the first state to declare it was seceding from the United States, fearing the spreading movement to abolish slavery and angry over the failure of the federal government to enforce the Fugitive Slave Acts.[3] Over the next seven months, ten other states seceded.[4] The Civil War this caused lasted until 1865.

AMENDMENT 13

(Ratified December 6, 1865)

Section 1. Neither slavery nor involuntary servitude, except as a punishment for crime whereof the party shall have been duly convicted, shall exist within the United States, or any place subject to their jurisdiction.

Section 2. Congress shall have power to enforce this article by appropriate legislation.

AMENDMENT 14

(Ratified July 9, 1868)

All persons born

The Thirteenth Amendment outlawed slavery in the United States; the southern states wanted to keep slavery.

During the final months of the Civil War, Congress passed the Thirteenth Amendment, which abolished slavery. The amendment had to be ratified by three-quarters of the states. With the Civil War only just ended, many southern states were run by "Reconstruction Governments" controlled by northern interests. That, and pressure from President Andrew Johnson, got the necessary number of states to ratify the amendment. Georgia pushed the amendment over the threshold on December 6, 1865, becoming the twenty-seventh state to ratify it.[5] Other states took much longer. Mississippi didn't fully ratify the amendment until 2013.[6]

This illustration shows the celebrations in the House of Representatives after it passed the Thirteenth Amendment on January 31, 1865.

During the ratification of the Thirteenth Amendment, members of southern governments were concerned the people they had once enslaved would be able to vote.[7] President Andrew Johnson left the decision about what legal rights the free black people would have to the states and didn't offer them any role in the Reconstruction happening around them. He even returned all lands seized by the Union to the white people who had once enslaved them.[8] In response, many of the southern states passed "Black

Codes" that restricted the rights of black people and forced many back onto plantations as laborers, enslaving them in all but name.[9]

The Fourteenth Amendment

In reaction to the bad acts of the southern states, Congress passed the Civil Rights Bill of 1866. Andrew Johnson attempted to veto it, but Congress overrode his veto on April 9, 1866—the first time a Congress had ever overridden a presidential veto on a major law. The Civil Rights Act of 1866 declared that everyone born in the United States—*except* "Indians"—was a citizen with full and equal benefit of the law.[10]

After the attempted veto, the Congress took no chances and put together the Fourteenth Amendment, which used language very similar to the Civil Rights Act of 1866. The Fourteenth Amendment says how southern war debts will be handled and that people who engaged in "rebellion or other crime" would not be allowed to vote.[11] It also says that states that disenfranchised male citizens who were eligible to vote would be punished with reduced representation in Congress.[12]

Enraged by the actions of the southern states, voters of the North rejected Andrew Johnson's policies in the election of 1866, electing a solidly Republican and abolitionist Congress. The Congress took over the Reconstruction of the South with the strict Reconstruction Act of 1867.[13] Part of the Reconstruction Act of 1867 required the southern states to ratify both the Thirteenth Amendment (if they hadn't already) and the Fourteenth Amendment if they wanted representation in Congress again.[14]. On July 28, 1868, the Fourteenth Amendment was ratified by the states.

The Fifteenth Amendment

In 1868, the year the Fourteenth Amendment was ratified, only eight states in the abolitionist North allowed black men to vote. In the South, suffrage

The Indian Citizenship Act

The Fourteenth Amendment—and many other laws that affected citizenship rights—specifically excluded Native Americans. While many Native Americans had and still have separate nations they are members of, they were still surrounded by the United States and felt the effects of the laws Congress enacted.[15]

In 1924, the Indian Citizenship Act was passed, granting all Native Americans dual citizenship in their nation and in the United States[16,17]—though the rights of citizenship were left up to the states. In 1957, Native Americans gained the right to vote in all states.[18] State efforts to deny Native American voting rights are still happening today, in many forms.[19]

for black men was only assured by the presence of the Union Army.[20] With black people now full citizens, the three-fifths compromise of the original Constitution, which said black people would only be counted as "three-fifths" of a person in the census that determined how many representatives each state got, was officially over. The southern states would have a much higher official population, and therefore more representatives,[21] making the ability of black men to vote or the suppression of that vote very valuable to politicians.

The Fifteenth Amendment faced much debate in Congress. Some of the more radical members wanted to ban laws that suppressed voting and protect the voting rights of citizens who were not born in the United States. Representatives from the North and West wanted to be able to deny the vote to foreign-born people, to prevent Chinese people and other ethnic minorities from voting. Many Republicans wanted to make sure they could keep denying the vote to people who had supported the Confederacy.[22]

Politicians were wary of allowing black men to vote, given blacks would
likely vote against the men who had held them in slavery.

The compromise produced a very simple amendment: "The right of citizens of the United States to vote shall not be denied or abridged by the United States or by any State on account of race, color, or previous condition of servitude. Congress shall have the power to enforce this article by appropriate legislation."

On paper, it ensured the rights of men of every race to vote. In reality, there was plenty of room for states to prevent people from voting.

3

Expanding the Vote

On March 31, 1776, Abigail Adams wrote to her husband, future President John Adams, "And, by the way, in the new code of laws which I suppose it will be necessary for you to make, I desire you would remember the ladies and be more generous and favorable to them than your ancestors. Do not put such unlimited power into the hands of the husbands. Remember, all men would be tyrants if they could. If particular care and attention is not paid to the ladies, we are determined to foment a rebellion, and will not hold ourselves bound by any laws in which we have no voice or representation."[1]

John Adams and his fellows forgot, ignored, or actively took away the few voting rights "the ladies" had at the founding of the United States, but the ladies themselves didn't forget. And in time, they did "foment a rebellion" as Abigail Adams had promised.

The Nineteenth Amendment

When the Fourteenth Amendment was ratified, it affirmed the rights of black men and women as citizens of the United States. It also added the first mention of gender into the Constitution: "But when the right to vote in any election… is denied to any of the male inhabitants of such State…" can be found in section 2 of the amendment.

Women had been extremely active in the abolitionist movement, and many abolitionist women also wanted more rights for women under the Constitution. The inclusion of gender in the Fourteenth Amendment, showing that only men were considered as voters, split support among those women when the Fifteenth Amendment was proposed the next year. Elizabeth Cady Stanton, a leader in the women's rights movement, said, "If the word 'male' be inserted, it will take us a century at least to get it out."

She and Susan B. Anthony objected to the Fifteenth Amendment on those grounds. Lucy Stone, another activist for women's suffrage, disagreed because she thought women would win the vote soon anyway.[2] Frederick Douglass, a black reformer committed to both abolition and women's suffrage,[3] publicly disagreed with Stanton and Anthony because he believed black men needed voting rights first because of the prejudice and violence they

Abigail Adams warned her husband John to not forget women when it came to making the laws of the new land; women, she felt, also required a voice in the nation, if they were meant to live in it.

faced.[4] The ratification of the Fifteenth Amendment brought out a racist side to the fight for women's suffrage, with activists like Stanton saying that black men weren't ready for the vote and using racial slurs.[5] Other white women fought alongside black women, like Sojourner Truth and later Ida B. Wells-Barnett, to secure the vote for all women.[6]

After a failed attempt at a constitutional amendment in 1886, activists started working on a state-by-state strategy. By 1896, Colorado, Utah, and Idaho had changed their state Constitutions to allow women to vote. By 1918, seventeen more states and territories followed that example.[7]

As the 1800s became the 1900s, women began to argue that they deserved the vote because they were different from men and would make different legislative decisions.[8] The Temperance Movement, which aimed to ban alcohol in the United States, supported giving women the right to vote because they would use their new power to prohibit alcohol.[9]

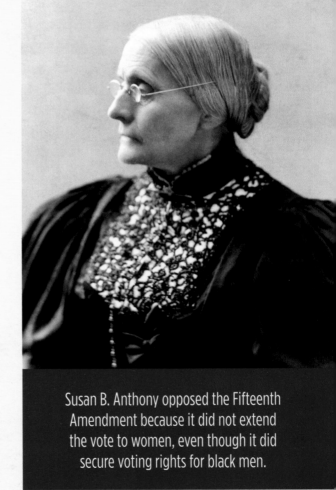

Susan B. Anthony opposed the Fifteenth Amendment because it did not extend the vote to women, even though it did secure voting rights for black men.

White supremacists like Belle Kearney argued that giving women the right to vote would ensure white supremacy through elections.[10] That black women would not be allowed to vote was implicit.

On March 3, 1913, five thousand women, including activist Helen Keller, paraded in Washington, D.C. to demand the right to vote before Woodrow Wilson's inauguration.[11] Initially against suffrage for women, President Wilson changed his mind over the next five years and supported an attempt at a constitutional amendment in 1918.[12]

The next year, the amendment passed and was sent to the states for ratification. Most of the southern states rejected the amendment, leaving it one state short. On August 18, 1920, Tennessee ratified the Nineteenth amendment 49–48.[13] The right of women of all races to vote was made official on August 26, 1920,[14] though it was subject to the whims of the states, just as the voting rights of black men had been.

The Seneca Falls Convention

The first women's rights convention in the United States was held in Seneca Falls, New York, in July 19–20 of 1848.[15] Eleven resolutions about the rights of women came out of the Seneca Falls Convention. The only resolution not passed unanimously was, "Resolved, That it is the duty of the women in this country to secure to themselves their sacred right to elective franchise."[16] Frederick Douglass, one of the few men in attendance, helped convince the convention to pass the resolution.[17]

The Twenty-Sixth Amendment

When the Constitution was originally written, the voting age had been twenty-one. Yet also since the beginning of the Constitution, men had been sent to war far younger. After the Civil War, delegates to New York's constitutional convention tried to lower the voting age to eighteen but were stopped. One delegate noted in frustration, "We hold men at 18 liable to the draft and require them to peril their lives on the battlefield."[18]

In the 1960s, young men could be drafted into war but could not yet vote. Many burned their draft cards in protest. The Twenty-sixth Amendment lowered the voting age from twenty-one to eighteen.

That age difference, between when men could be drafted to go to war and when they could vote for the officials who declared wars, continued to be on the minds of people. President Dwight D. Eisenhower, who had been a five-star general during World War II, talked about it in his second State of the Union address in 1954.[19]

During the 1960s, America was in the midst of the Vietnam War. Soldiers were drafted, mostly from poor and working-class families.[20] The war became increasingly unpopular as time went on,[21] with widespread national protests starting in 1965.[22] Student activists brought back a slogan from World War II: "Old enough to fight, old enough to vote."[23]

In April of 1970, Congress tried to lower the voting age to eighteen legislatively when they extended the Voting Rights Act of 1965. In the case *Oregon v. Mitchell*, the Supreme Court ruled that the federal government could change the voting age for federal elections, but not for state and local elections.[24] A constitutional amendment was necessary.

The Congress acted swiftly, worried about confusion in the next election and pressed by ongoing protests from young men and women. In March of 1971, the Senate voted unanimously and House overwhelmingly in favor of passing the Twenty-Sixth Amendment. Two months later, the fastest any amendment has ever gone through the states, the Twenty-Sixth Amendment was ratified and signed by President Nixon. Eleven million more people could suddenly vote.[25]

4

What Is a Vote Worth When It Can't Be Cast?

In theory, by 1868, male American citizens of all races could vote. As of 1920, female American citizens of all races could vote as well. The administration of elections and voter registration was still left up to the states. Almost as soon as voting rights were granted by the federal government, states that had once tried to secede from the union moved to take them away with tricks that looked legal on paper.[1] This voter suppression raised a question that still haunts America today—does someone really have the right to vote if they're not allowed to cast a ballot?

Voter Suppression in the Era of Jim Crow

Beginning in the 1890s, governments in the southern states began passing laws that mandated segregation, legally forcing nonwhite people who lived there to use inferior public services or occupy inferior public spaces. These laws were called "Jim Crow" laws, taking their name from a racist insult directed at black people.[2]

This was considered legal at the time under the theory that nonwhite people had access to "separate but equal" facilities and services. For example, drinking fountains were labeled for "Whites only" and "Colored," and if a

Demonstrations for equal voting rights, equal pay, and an end to police brutality have always been a part of America.

nonwhite person was caught using the "Whites only" drinking fountain, they would be punished under the law—or worse.[3]

Many decades later, Chief Justice Earl Warren of the Supreme Court would destroy the idea of "separate but equal" in *Brown v. Board of Education*, the case that forced desegregation of schools, by writing, "Separate educational facilities are inherently unequal."[4]

"Jim Crow" laws were also aimed at the voting rights of nonwhite people in the South. There were several common ways the laws prevented people from voting, including:

- **Poll Taxes:** Laws were passed in many states that required voters to pay a fee before they could cast a ballot. Since black people were generally poorer than white people, the law hit them the hardest. This also prevented poor white people from voting, but some states carved out "grandfather clauses" that allowed poor white people to vote without paying.[5,6]

- **Literacy Tests:** These laws required people to pass a test if they wanted to register to vote. These tests could be difficult quizzes on the federal or state constitution, or they could be nonsensical and unanswerable questions like, how many bubbles were in a bar of soap. Supporters claimed that literacy tests were to ensure that voters were educated and informed. However, these tests were aimed mostly at poor people, immigrants, and in the South, black people. The tests were also given unfairly—the registration official would choose what questions were asked and how they would grade the tests, which meant they could give nonwhite voters more difficult questions or interpret correct answers as wrong.[7,8,9]

- **Voter Purges:** The government could take names off the official list of registered voters. This meant that when someone arrived to vote, they wouldn't be on the list and wouldn't be given a ballot. White officials often took the names of black voters off the lists. The voters wouldn't know they had been removed until it was too late to vote, and then they'd have to try to register again after the election.[10]

- **Disenfranchisement for "moral turpitude:"** As early as 1894, states began passing laws that would allow them to take the right to vote from anyone who committed even a minor crime. Black people were often targeted for arrest, sometimes on false charges—and one arrest could lead to a person losing their right to vote forever. Similar laws were also passed in northern states.[11,12]

When racist laws failed to prevent black people from voting, they faced intimidation and violence from white people when they tried to exercise their rights. As early as 1878, Congress no longer allowed the federal soldiers occupying the South to protect black voters. By 1894, they had also taken away all the money that had once funded federal marshals to protect these voters.[13] With no protection, black people were regularly threatened or subjected to violence when they tried to vote and targeted for intimidation by white supremacist organizations like the Ku Klux Klan. Public officials and police ignored the violence and threats or even participated in it themselves.[14,15,16]

In the 1960s, John Lewis (*left*) marched in Alabama with the Freedom Riders and was beaten and injured for his efforts. Today, Lewis is a representative in Congress, continuing the fight for equality.

The Selma Injunction

The Civil Rights Movement wasn't that long ago. Many of its heroes are still alive today. Before he was a representative for Georgia, Congressman John Lewis helped fight for the right of black people to vote across the South. On July 6, 1964, in Selma, Alabama, he led fifty people who wanted to register to vote to the courthouse. All of them were arrested. On March 7, 1965, he led six hundred peaceful protesters across the Edmund Pettis Bridge in Selma, where they were attacked by white state troopers, one of whom fractured Congressman Lewis's skull. In his time protesting for voting rights and other civil rights, the congressman has been arrested over forty times—and he's still peacefully fighting today.[17,18,19]

The Voting Rights Act of 1965

The oppression that African Americans and other nonwhite people faced throughout the United States after the Civil War was not something they simply accepted. Racist laws were fought in the courts and protested in the streets in the decades that followed the end of Reconstruction. By the 1950s the grass-roots organizations reached a critical mass and became the Civil Rights Movement.[20]

The battle for equal rights was fought on many fronts. One important aspect was the demand that the suppression of black voters had to end. It was dangerous work; the Ku Klux Klan burned twenty black churches in Mississippi in the summer of 1964 alone. On June 21 that summer, three young men who volunteered to help with voter registration and other civil rights efforts in Mississippi were arrested by the local police and then murdered after their release. Their names were Michael Schwener, James Chaney, and Andrew Goodman.[21] A little less than nine months later on March 7, 1965, civil rights workers were attacked by white law enforcement officers on the Edmund Pettis Bridge in Selma, Alabama, as they protested

John Lewis, chairman of the Student Nonviolent Coordinating Committee, is beaten by state troopers during a civil rights march in March 1967.

the continued suppression of black voters. The violence was broadcast on television, sparking outrage and sympathy across the country.[22]

President Lyndon B. Johnson called for a strong voting rights law. He used the shock and revulsion at the violence of the white law enforcement officers to break down opposition from southern politicians in Congress.[23] Congressional hearings showed that existing antidiscrimination laws weren't enough to stop the states from suppressing voters' rights. Congress also determined it was necessary to require states with a history of voter suppression to have their laws approved by the Department of Justice *before* they could go into effect,[24] which was later called preclearance.

The Voting Rights Act did not stop all violence against black voters. But it ended the laws that let state governments prevent them from registering and voting. A year and a half later, nine of the thirteen southern states had over fifty percent of their black citizens registered to vote.[25]

5

Can Every Adult in America Vote?

Between the constitutional amendments and laws like the Indian Citizenship Act and the Voting Rights Act every person over the age of eighteen should be able to vote in America. But is that really how things are?

Voting in Nonstates

The United States has territories that spread across the Caribbean and the Pacific, including Puerto Rico and Guam. People in those territories can vote in local elections, but they can't vote for President of the United States. Each territory has one delegate that can go to the House of Representatives, and these delegates aren't allowed to vote on legislation. They don't have any representation in the Senate.[1]

The situation for Washington, DC, is similar. Washington, DC, only gets a single delegate in the House of Representatives. Due to the passage of the Twenty-Third Amendment in 1961, its citizens can vote for president, and they get the same number of electoral votes as the least populous state—three.[2] Congress also has direct oversight on Washington, DC, which means that people elected from distant states can—and have—overruled laws enacted by the local city council.[3]

Washington, DC, is not a state and has only a single delegate in the House of Representatives. The Twenty-third Amendment ensures that Washington can vote for president and assign electoral votes.

How Does a Territory Become a State?

Article IV, Section 3 of the Constitution says that new states are admitted to the United States by Congress. Normally, territories ask their residents to vote on whether they want to be a state, then have a convention and write a state constitution. If the residents approve the state constitution, it's sent to Congress for approval. Congress then issues a joint resolution (similar to a bill) to bring the new state into the country and the President approves it.[4]

In 2017, a referendum in Puerto Rico about statehood passed overwhelmingly, though voter turnout was low.[5] President Trump said he would not support statehood for Puerto Rico, because he didn't like the Mayor of San Juan, Carmen Yulín Cruz, who was critical of federal disaster relief response when hurricane Maria devastated the island in 2017.[6]

Felony Disenfranchisement

In 2018, Florida voters passed "Amendment Four," which automatically restored voting rights to people who have been convicted of a felony, served their prison sentence, and completed probation. Murderers and sex offenders are, however, excluded.[7] Iowa and Kentucky still have laws that automatically and permanently take away the voting rights of anyone who has been convicted of a felony. All but two states place some restrictions on the voting rights of people who have been convicted of felonies.[8]

Many felony disenfranchisement laws have roots in the Jim Crow era, when fairly minor crimes were made into felonies as an excuse to deny black citizens voting rights.[9] In Florida, 1.5 million people had their voting rights taken away before the law changed. Across America more than six million still do. Felony disenfranchisement can affect people of all races, but it affects black people at higher rates across all of the states.[10]

Many states require identification for voting, but the process is often convoluted, targeting minority voters who don't have easy access to acquiring identification.

Modern Voter Suppression

In America today, election laws are still under the control of individual states. Some states, like Colorado, automatically send all registered voters mail-in ballots. Fifteen states and Washington, DC, have laws that automatically register everyone to vote.[11] Other states do not make registering or voting so easy.

Shelby County v. Holder

In April of 2010, Shelby County, Alabama, filed a court case challenging the part of the Voting Rights Act that required preclearance of election laws from states with a history of racist voter suppression. In 2013, the Supreme Court decided in favor of Shelby County in the case *Shelby County v. Holder*.[12]

Since the court case, many of the states that had required preclearance passed new laws, especially Voter ID laws. These laws were often challenged by the Department of Justice under President Obama, but have not been under President Trump.[13,14]

Voter Registration Problems

In 2018, the Secretary of State in Georgia, Brian Kemp, was running to be governor. He did not recuse himself from running the election, so he was in charge of the voters and election rules for his own election. He instated an "exact match" program, which allowed him to place new voter registrations on hold if there was a typo or different punctuation in voter information. Over fifty-three thousand new registrations were on hold because of the policy. The applications were disproportionately for minority voters trying to register, and he was sued over it.[15] Other states have made new rules on voter registration, such as Florida, which requires registration forms to be turned in within two days, that have made voter registration drives much more difficult.[16]

Voter ID Laws

By 2018, thirty-eight states had laws that required a voter show some form of ID when they vote. Some states have easy voter ID requirements that allow things like student ID cards, but other states require more specific ID.[17]

Voter ID laws have been criticized because strict ID requirements can make it very difficult for some people to get the required ID. The people who find it most difficult tend to be minorities and the elderly, often because they don't have the exact documentation they need.[18,19] In one example, a ninety-six-year-old black woman who voted during the Jim Crow era was denied the required ID card because her last name on her birth certificate didn't match her married name, and she didn't have her marriage license.[20] Research done by the *Washington Post* shows that Voter ID Laws suppress voting by minorities.[21]

In October 2018, the Supreme Court allowed a North Dakota law that doesn't permit people to use a PO Box as their address for registering. Many Native Americans use PO Boxes to register to vote. The people who made the North Dakota law and most other Voter ID Laws say it will combat voter fraud.[22] Multiple studies have shown that voter fraud of this kind is extremely rare. Two such studies from Arizona State University showed only ten cases of voter fraud occurred between 2000–2012 in the entire United States.[23]

Long Lines, Closed Polls

States and counties sometimes close or move polling places where people vote. This can be because not enough people use the polling place or because there isn't enough money to keep all of the polling places open. Polling places closing can lead to extremely long lines, however. Maricopa County in Arizona, which used to require preclearance under the Voting Rights Act, closed seventy percent of their polling places since 2013, causing waits of five hours and lines that went around the block. In the years between *Shelby County v. Holder* and 2016, 868 polling places in counties that had once required preclearance under the Voting Rights Act closed.[24]

Voter Purges

States can and do remove people from their list of registered voters for many reasons, such as being registered in multiple states or if there is a problem with their address. However, as in the example of the letters sent by the Harris County Registrar, people can be removed from the voter rolls wrongly.[25] The Brennan Center says that thousands of people have been wrongly purged from voter rolls since 2015, often with little or no notice that they will no longer be able to vote.[26]

Voters have been removed from states that were once required preclearance at higher rate than other states.[27] In Georgia, more than a million voters that the secretary of state said were inactive have been removed since 2010.[28] In 2016, a program called the Interstate Voter Registration Crosscheck Program

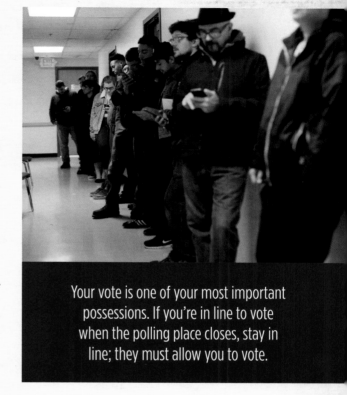

Your vote is one of your most important possessions. If you're in line to vote when the polling place closes, stay in line; they must allow you to vote.

produced lists of voters they claimed were registered in more than one state and should have their registration purged. *Rolling Stone* found the listed voters were more often young people and racial minorities.[29] *The Washington Post* found in 2017 that ninety-nine percent of the names the Crosscheck Program sent to Iowa should not have been listed.[30]

The right to vote in America has been something that people have fought, bled, and even died for since the founding of the country. It's the greatest power that any single citizen has, the small but important part each person has in the government of the United States, and that's the reason people are still fighting for it today.

As former Secretary of State Hillary Clinton said: "Voting is the most precious right of every citizen, and we have a moral obligation to ensure the integrity of our voting process."

Chapter Notes

Introduction

1. "Harris County May Have Violated Federal Election Law, Expert Says," *Texas Monthly*, August 24, 2018, https://www.texasmonthly.com/news/harris-county-may-violated-federal-election-law-expert-says/

2. "One Republican Official Challenged Thousands of Voter Registrations in His County. It Could Happen Elsewhere." *Huffington Post*, September 17, 2018, https://www.huffingtonpost.com/entry/republican-challenge-voter-registration-houston_us_5b9fb69ce4b046313fbd65d3

3. Riley, Nicolas. "Voter Challengers," Brennan Center for Justice, https://www.brennan-center.org/sites/default/files/legacy/publications/Voter_Challengers.pdf

4. "State and County QuickFacts: Harris County, Texas," U.S. Census Bureau, https://www.webcitation.org/606IF616l?url=http://quickfacts.census.gov/qfd/states/48/48201.html

5. "How Houston has become the most diverse place in America," *LA Times*, May 9, 2017, http://www.latimes.com/nation/la-na-houston-diversity-2017-htmlstory.html

6. "Directory of Representatives," United States House of Representatives, https://www.house.gov/representatives

7. "Federal judge: Texas is violating national voter registration law," *The Texas Tribune*, April 3, 2018, https://www.texastribune.org/2018/04/03/federal-judge-hands-texas-loss-voter-registration-lawsuit/

8. "A Court Strikes Down Texas's Voter ID Law for the Fifth Time," *The Atlantic*, Ausuts 24, 2017, https://www.theatlantic.com/politics/archive/2017/08/a-court-strikes-down-texass-voter-id-law-for-the-fifth-time/537792/

9. "'Shelby County': One Year Later," Brennan Center for Justice, http://www.brennancenter.org/analysis/shelby-county-one-year-later

Chapter One: Voting Rights at the Founding of the United States

1. "Athens," The British Museum, http://www.ancientgreece.co.uk/athens/home_set.html

2. "Election," Britannica.com, https://www.britannica.com/topic/election-political-science

3. "Articles of Confederation," Britannica.com, https://www.britannica.com/topic/Articles-of-Confederation

4. "Articles of Confederation 1777–1781," Office of the Historian, https://history.state.gov/milestones/1776-1783/articles

5. "Articles of Confederation," History.com, https://www.history.com/topics/early-us/articles-of-confederation

6. "The Constitutional Convention debates and the Anti-Federalist Papers," American History from Revolution to Reconstruction and beyond, http://www.let.rug.nl/usa/documents/1786-1800/the-anti-federalist-papers/

7. Ibid.

8. "Comparing the Articles and the Constitution," usconstitution.net, https://www.usconstitution.net/constconart.html

9. "State Houses Elect Senators," United States Senate, https://www.senate.gov/artandhistory/history/minute/State_Houses_Elect_Senators.htm

10. "James Madison, Note to His Speech on the Right to Suffrage," The Founder's Constitution, http://press-pubs.uchicago.edu/founders/documents/v1ch16s26.html

11. "Elections… the American Way," Library of Congress, https://www.loc.gov/teachers/classroommaterials/presentationsandactivities/presentations/elections/founders-and-the-vote.html

12. "The Constitution of the United States: A Transcription," National Archives, https://www.archives.gov/founding-docs/constitution-transcript

13. "Voting in Early America," Colonial Williamsburg, http://www.history.org/foundation/journal/spring07/elections.cfm

14. "Expansion of Rights and Liberties – The Right of Suffrage," The Charters of Freedom accessed via the Wayback Machine, https://web.archive.org/web/20160706144856/http://www.archives.gov/exhibits/charters/charters_of_freedom_13.html

15. "Women's Rights After the American Revolution," womenhistoryblog.com, http://www.womenhistoryblog.com/2013/06/womens-rights-after-american-revolution.html

16. "The State Where Women Voted Long Before the 19th Amendment," History.com, https://www.history.com/news/the-state-where-women-voted-long-before-the-19th-amendment

17. "For a Few Decades in the 18th Century, Women and African-Americans Could Vote in New Jersey," Smithsonian.com, https://www.smithsonianmag.com/smart-news/why-black-people-and-women-lost-vote-new-jersey-180967186/

18. Smith, Eric Ledell. "The End of Black Voting Rights in Pennsylvania: African Americans and the Pennsylvania Constitutional Convention of 1837-1838," *Pennsylvania History: A Journal of Mid-Atlantic Studies*, Vol. 65 No. 3, Penn State University Press. https://www.jstor.org/stable/27774118?seq=1#page_scan_tab_contents

Chapter Two: Voting Rights for (Almost) All Men

1. Engerman, Stanley L. and Sokoloff, Kenneth L. "The Evolution of Suffrage Institutions in the New World," February 2005, yale.edu, http://economics.yale.edu/sites/default/files/files/Workshops-Seminars/Economic-History/sokoloff-050406.pdf

2. "Quaker Activism," PBS.org, http://www.pbs.org/opb/historydetectives/feature/quaker-activism/

3. "Confederate States of America – Declaration of Immediate Causes Which Induce and Justify the Secession of South Carolina from the Federal Union," *The Avalon Project*, http://avalon.law.yale.edu/19th_century/csa_scarsec.asp

4. "Confederate States of America," History.com, https://www.history.com/topics/american-civil-war/confederate-states-of-america

5. "13th Amendment to the Constitution of the United States," Smithsonian - National Museum of African American History and Culture, https://nmaahc.si.edu/blog-post/13th-amendment-constitution-united-states

6. "After 148 years, Mississippi finally ratifies 13th Amendment, which banned slavery," *CBS News*, https://www.cbsnews.com/news/after-148-years-mississippi-finally-ratifies-13th-amendment-which-banned-slavery/

7. Du Bois, W.E.B. *Black Reconstruction in America: An Essay Toward a History of the Part Which Black Folk Played in the Attempt to Reconstruct Democracy in America, 1860-1880*, 1935

8. "Presidential Reconstruction," America's Reconstruction: People and Politics After the Civil War, http://www.digitalhistory.uh.edu/exhibits/reconstruction/section4/section4_presrecon.html

9. "Slavery by Another Name," PBS.org, http://www.pbs.org/tpt/slavery-by-another-name/themes/black-codes/

10. "The Civil Rights Bill of 1866," United States House of Representatives: History, Art & Archives, http://history.house.gov/Historical-Highlights/1851-1900/The-Civil-Rights-Bill-of-1866/

11. "14th Amendment," Legal Information Institute, https://www.law.cornell.edu/constitution/amendmentxiv

12. Foner, Eric. *Reconstruction: America's Unfinished Revolution*, 1863-1877. Harper Collins, 2011.

13. "Reconstruction," History.com, https://www.history.com/topics/american-civil-war/reconstruction

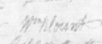

14. "14th Amendment," History.com, https://www.history.com/topics/black-history/fourteenth-amendment

15. "The Indian Citizenship Act," History.com, https://www.history.com/this-day-in-history/the-indian-citizenship-act

16. Ibid.

17. "Repatriation, Land, and Sovereignty: The Indian Citizenship Act (1924) and the Indian Reorganization Act (1934)," Vassar Repatriation Blog, https://pages.vassar.edu/theirsorours/2015/02/10/repatriation-land-and-sovereignty-the-indian-citizenship-act-1924-and-the-indian-reorganization-act-1934/

18. Rollings, Willard Hughes. "Citizenship and Suffrage: The Native American Struggle for Civil Rights in the American West, 1830-1965," *Nevada Law Journal*, Vol. 5: Iss. 1, 2004. https://core.ac.uk/download/pdf/10678666.pdf

19. "Faced with discrimination, Native Americans work hard to gain voting power," *The Christian Science Monitor*, October 1, 2018, https://www.csmonitor.com/USA/Politics/2018/1001/Faced-with-discrimination-Native-Americans-work-hard-to-gain-voting-power

20. Ibid.

21. Nelson, William E. *The Fourteenth Amendment: From Political Principle to Judicial Doctrine*. Cambridge, Massachusetts: Harvard University Press, 1988.

22. "Fifteenth Amendment (Framing and Ratification)," Encyclopedia of the American Constitution, accessed via highbeam.com, https://www.highbeam.com/doc/1G2-3425000965.html

Chapter Three: Expanding the Vote

1. "Letter from Abigail Adams to John Adams, 31 March – 5 April 1776," Massachusetts Historical Society, https://www.masshist.org/digitaladams/archive/doc?id=L17760331aa

2. "14th and 15th Amendment," National Women's History Museum, http://www.crusade-forthevote.org/14-15-amendments/

3. "Frederick Douglass," NPS.gov, https://www.nps.gov/wori/learn/historyculture/frederick-douglass.htm

4. "(1888) Frederick Douglass on Woman Suffrage," BlackPast.org, https://blackpast.org/1888-frederick-douglass-woman-suffrage

5. "In America; Stanton and Anthony," *The New York Times*, July 4, 1999, https://www.nytimes.com/1999/07/04/opinion/in-america-stanton-and-anthony.html

6. "Women's Suffrage Leaders Left Out Black Women," *Teen Vogue,* August 18, 2017, https://www.teenvogue.com/story/womens-suffrage-leaders-left-out-black-women

7. "19th Amendment," History.com, https://www.history.com/topics/womens-history/19th-amendment-1

8. Ibid.

9. "Abolition, Women's Rights, and Temperance Movements," NPS.gov, https://www.nps.gov/wori/learn/historyculture/abolition-womens-rights-and-temperance-movements.htm

10. "'Durable White Supremacy': Belle Kearney Puts Black Men in Their Place," History Matters: The U.S. Survey Course on the Web, http://historymatters.gmu.edu/d/5317/

11. "The Original Women's March on Washington and the Suffragists Who Paved the Way," Smithsonian.com, https://www.smithsonianmag.com/history/original-womens-march-washington-and-suffragists-who-paved-way-180961869/

12. Ibid.

13. Ibid.

14. "19th Amendment to the U.S. Constitution: Women's Right to Vote (1920)," ourdocuments.gov, https://www.ourdocuments.gov/doc.php?flash=false&doc=63

15. "Seneca Falls Convention," History.com, https://www.history.com/topics/womens-rights/seneca-falls-convention

16. "Declaration of Sentiments," Seneca Falls, NY, 19-20 July 1848. *History of Woman Suffrage*, http://utc.iath.virginia.edu/abolitn/abwmat.html

17. Staples, Brent. "How the Suffrage Movement Betrayed Black Women," *The New York Times,* July 28, 2018, https://www.nytimes.com/2018/07/28/opinion/sunday/suffrage-movement-racism-black-women.html

18. Saldin, Robert P. *War, the American State, and Politics Since 1898.* Cambridge, NY: Cambridge University Press, 2011.

19. "Dwight D. Eisenhower's Second State of the Union Address," wikisource.org, https://en.wikisource.org/wiki/Dwight_D._Eisenhower%27s_Second_State_of_the_Union_Address

20. "Vietnam War Draft," thevietnamwar.info, https://thevietnamwar.info/vietnam-war-draft/

21. Lunch, William L. and Sperlich, Peter W. "American Public Opinion and the War in Vietnam." *The Western Political Quarterly,* Vol. 32 No. 1, March 1979. https://www.jstor.org/stable/447561?seq=1#page_scan_tab_contents

22. "Vietnam War Protests," History.com, https://www.history.com/topics/vietnam-war/vietnam-war-protests

23. "Records of Rights Vote: "Old Enough to Fight, Old Enough to Vote," National Archives, https://prologue.blogs.archives.gov/2013/11/13/records-of-rights-vote-old-enough-to-fight-old-enough-to-vote/

24. "Supreme Court partially upholds voting rights for 18-year-olds, Dec. 21, 1970," politico.com, https://www.politico.com/story/2017/12/21/this-day-in-politics-dec-21-1970-301739

25. "The 26th Amendment," History.com, https://www.history.com/topics/united-states-constitution/the-26th-amendment

Chapter Four: What Is a Vote Worth When It Can't Be Cast?

1. "White Only: Jim Crow in America," Smithsonian National Museum of American History, http://americanhistory.si.edu/brown/history/1-segregated/white-only-1.html

2. "Jim Crow Law," Briannica.com, https://www.britannica.com/event/Jim-Crow-law

3. "Jim Crow Laws," PBS.org, https://www.pbs.org/wgbh/americanexperience/features/freedom-riders-jim-crow-laws/

4. *Brown v. Board of Education*, 374 U.S. 483 (1954), accessed via Legal Information Institute, https://www.law.cornell.edu/supremecourt/text/347/483

5. "Poll Tax," Britannica.com, https://www.britannica.com/topic/poll-tax

6. "Poll Taxes," Smithsonian National Museum of American History, http://americanhistory.si.edu/democracy-exhibition/vote-voice/keeping-vote/state-rules-federal-rules/poll-taxes

7. "The Rise and Fall of Jim Crow," thirteen.org, https://www.thirteen.org/wnet/jimcrow/voting_literacy.html

8. "Civil Rights Movement Voting Rights: Are You 'Qualified' to Vote? Take a 'Literacy Test' to Find Out," Civil Rights Movement Veterans, https://www.crmvet.org/info/lithome.htm

9. "Literacy Tests," Smithsonian National Museum of American History, http://american-history.si.edu/democracy-exhibition/vote-voice/keeping-vote/state-rules-federal-rules/literacy-tests

10. "Voting Rights for Blacks and Poor Whites in the Jim Crow South," America's Black Holocaust Museum, https://abhmuseum.org/voting-rights-for-blacks-and-poor-whites-in-the-jim-crow-south/

11. Staples, Brent. "The Racist Origins of Felon Disenfranchisement," *The New York Times*, November 18, 2014, https://www.nytimes.com/2014/11/19/opinion/the-racist-origins-of-felon-disenfranchisement.html

12. Ibid.

13. "The Rise and Fall of Jim Crow: A National Struggle," thirteen.org, https://www.thirteen.org/wnet/jimcrow/struggle_congress.html

14. "Race and Voting in the Segregated South," Constitutional Rights Foundation, http://www.crf-usa.org/black-history-month/race-and-voting-in-the-segregated-south

15. "The Rise and Fall of Jim Crow: Jim Crow Stories," thirteen.org, https://www.thirteen.org/wnet/jimcrow/stories_org_kkk.html

16. Ibid.

17. "Selma to Montgomery March," The Martin Luther King, Jr. Research and Education Institute at Stanford, https://kinginstitute.stanford.edu/encyclopedia/selma-montgomery-march

18. "Civil Rights Movement History 1964 July-Dec," Civil Rights Movement Veterans, https://www.crmvet.org/tim/tim64c.htm#1964selmainj

19. "Biography of Congressman John Lewis," house.gov, https://johnlewis.house.gov/john-lewis/biography

20. "Civil Rights Movement," History.com, https://www.history.com/topics/black-history/civil-rights-movement

21. "Murder in Mississippi," PBS.org, https://www.pbs.org/wgbh/americanexperience/features/freedomsummer-murder/

22. "Voting Rights Act of 1965," The Martin Luther King, Jr. Research and Education Institute at Stanford, https://kinginstitute.stanford.edu/encyclopedia/voting-rights-act-1965

23. "Voting Rights Act of 1965," History.com, https://www.history.com/topics/black-history/voting-rights-act

24. "History of Federal Voting Rights Laws," United States Department of Justice, https://www.justice.gov/crt/history-federal-voting-rights-laws

25. "Voting Rights Act (1965)," ourdocuments.gov, https://www.ourdocuments.gov/doc.php?flash=false&doc=100

Chapter 5: Can Every Adult Vote in America?

1. "More than 4 million Americans don't have anyone to vote for them in Congress," *The Washington Post*, September 28, 2017, https://www.washingtonpost.com/graphics/2017/national/fair-representation/?noredirect=on&utm_term=.24d4e8aac85e

2. "Twenty-third Amendment," Britannica.com, https://www.britannica.com/topic/Twenty-third-Amendment

3. "Congress once ran the local D.C. government. GOP signals that it may do so again," *The Washington Post*, January 30, 2017, https://www.washingtonpost.com/local/dc-politics/congress-once-ran-the-local-dc-government--gop-signaling-it-may-do-so-again/2017/01/30/814f89a2-e71f-11e6-bf6f-301b6b443624_story.html?utm_term=.f83b34be9d30

4. "Admission of States to Union," u-s-history.com, https://www.u-s-history.com/pages/h928.html

5. "Puerto Rico's Plebiscite to Nowhere," *The Atlantic*, June 13, 2017, https://www.theatlantic.com/politics/archive/2017/06/puerto-rico-statehood-plebiscite-congress/530136/

6. "Trump an 'absolute no' on Puerto Rico statehood because of San Juan's 'horror show' of a mayor," *The Washington Post*, September 24, 2018, https://www.washingtonpost.com/politics/trump-an-absolute-no-on-puerto-rico-statehood-because-of-san-juans-horror-show-of-a-mayor/2018/09/24/897ec214-c021-11e8-9005-5104e9616c21_story.html?utm_term=.ed5d6cb1005f

7. Lopez, German. "Florida votes to restore ex-felon voting rights with Amendment 4," Vox.com, https://www.vox.com/policy-and-politics/2018/11/6/18052374/florida-amendment-4-felon-voting-rights-results

8. "Felony Disenfranchisement Laws (Map)," ACLU.org, https://www.aclu.org/issues/voting-rights/voter-restoration/felony-disenfranchisement-laws-map

9. "The 'Slave Power' Behind Florida's Felon Disenfranchisement," *The Atlantic*, February 4, 2018, https://www.theatlantic.com/politics/archive/2018/02/the-slave-power-behind-floridas-felon-disenfranchisement/552269/

10. "6 Million Lost Voters: State-Level Estimates of Felony Disenfranchisement, 2016," The Sentencing Project, https://www.sentencingproject.org/publications/6-million-lost-voters-state-level-estimates-felony-disenfranchisement-2016/

11. "Automatic Voter Registration," Brennan Center for Justice, https://www.brennancenter.org/analysis/automatic-voter-registration

12. *Shelby County v. Holder*, 570 U.S. 2 (2013), accessed via oyez.org, https://www.oyez.org/cases/2012/12-96

13. "How *Shelby County v. Holder* Broke America," *The Atlantic*, July 10, 2018, https://www.theatlantic.com/politics/archive/2018/07/how-shelby-county-broke-america/564707/

14. "The Effect of Shelby County v. Holder," Brennan Center for Justice, https://www.brennancenter.org/analysis/effects-shelby-county-v-holder

15. "The Georgia Voter Suppression Story Is Not Going Away," *Rolling Stone*, October 12, 2018, https://www.rollingstone.com/politics/politics-news/georgia-voter-suppression-brian-kemp-736817/

16. Lieberman, Denise. "Barriers to the Ballot Box: New Restrictions Underscore the Need for Voting Laws Enforcement," American Bar Association Human Rights Magazine, Vol. 39, Winter 2012, https://www.americanbar.org/publications/human_rights_magazine_home/2012_vol_39_/winter_2012_-_vote/barriers_to_the_ballotboxnewrestrictionsunderscoretheneedforvoti/

17. "Voter Identification Requirements | Voter ID Laws," National Conference of State Legislatures, http://www.ncsl.org/research/elections-and-campaigns/voter-id.aspx

18. "Getting a photo ID so you can vote is easy. Unless you're poor, black, Latino, or elderly," *The Washington Post*, May 23, 2016, https://www.washingtonpost.com/politics/courts_law/getting-a-photo-id-so-you-can-vote-is-easy-unless-youre-poor-black-latino-or-elderly/2016/05/23/8d5474ec-20f0-11e6-8690-f14ca9de2972_story.html?utm_term=.c2c28ec2daf4

19. "Voter Photo ID Laws Hit Older Americans Hard," AARP.org, https://www.aarp.org/politics-society/government-elections/info-01-2012/voter-id-laws-impact-older-americans.html

20. "96-year-old Woman Who Voted During Jim Crow Is Denited Photo ID," *Nashville Scene*, October 5, 2011, https://www.nashvillescene.com/news/pith-in-the-wind/article/13040146/96yearold-woman-who-voted-during-jim-crow-is-denied-photo-id

21. "Do voter identification laws suppress minority voting? Yes. We did the research," *The Washington Post*, February 15, 2017, https://www.washingtonpost.com/news/monkey-cage/wp/2017/02/15/do-voter-identification-laws-suppress-minority-voting-yes-we-did-the-research/?utm_term=.089b3998235b

22. "In Senate battleground, Native American voting rights activists fight back against voter ID restrictions," *The Washington Post*, October 12, 2018, https://www.washingtonpost.com/politics/in-senate-battleground-native-american-voting-rights-activists-fight-back-against-voter-id-restrictions/2018/10/12/7bc33ad2-cd60-11e8-a360-85875bac0b1f_story.html?utm_term=.78a25a832078

23. "Debunking the Voter Fraud Myth," Brennan Center for Justice, https://www.brennancenter.org/analysis/debunking-voter-fraud-myth

24. "There Are 868 Fewer Places to Vote in 2016 Because the Supreme Court Gutted the Voting Rights Act," *The Nation*, November 4, 2016, https://www.thenation.com/article/there-are-868-fewer-places-to-vote-in-2016-because-the-supreme-court-gutted-the-voting-rights-act/

25. "Harris County May Have Violated Federal Election Law, Expert Says," *Texas Monthly*, August 24, 2018, https://www.texasmonthly.com/news/harris-county-may-violated-federal-election-law-expert-says/

26. "Voter Purges: The Risks in 2018," Brennan Center for Justice, https://www.brennan-center.org/publication/voter-purges-risks-2018

27. "Voter purge frenzy after federal protections lifted, new report says," NBCnews.com, https://www.nbcnews.com/politics/politics-news/voter-roll-purges-surged-after-changes-voting-rights-act-new-n893056

28. Ibid.

29. "The GOP's Stealth War Against Voters," *Rolling Stone*, August 24, 2016, https://www.rollingstone.com/politics/politics-features/the-gops-stealth-war-against-voters-247905/

30. "The anti-voter-fraud program gets it wrong over 99 percent of the time. The GOP wants to take it nationwide," *The Washington Post*, July 20, 2017, https://www.washingtonpost.com/news/wonk/wp/2017/07/20/this-anti-voter-fraud-program-gets-it-wrong-over-99-of-the-time-the-gop-wants-to-take-it-nationwide/?utm_term=.40409e2b4b5e

Glossary

abolished Formally ended something, normally a law, entity, or practice.

abolitionist Generally, someone who wants to end a practice or legal entity. In history, "abolitionists" normally refers to people who wanted to end slavery.

disenfranchisement Having your right to vote taken away.

disproportionately When the effect of something is too big or small compared to the reality. For example: thirty percent of the people who live in the state aren't white. The state makes a new law and seventy percent of the people that law affects are not white. The law disproportionately affects nonwhite people.

draft To require or force someone to serve in the military.

polling place Where people go to vote in person during elections.

preclearance Requiring states or counties to have laws checked by the Department of Justice before the laws can go into effect. The Supreme Court case *Shelby County v. Holder* ended preclearance for states and counties with a history of racist voting laws.

ratify To sign or give formal consent for a legal document, like a treaty or a constitutional amendment.

recuse To remove yourself from a case or official activity as a judge or official because you a have a conflict of interest or can't be fair.

registrar The person responsible for keeping and registering official records.

secede To withdraw formally from a union.

segregation The separation of racial groups by law and force.

suffrage The right to vote in elections.

voter fraud When someone casts illegal votes, either because they are not supposed to be able to vote or because they are voting multiple times.

voter suppression Preventing people in certain groups from voting as a way to try to change who will win an election.

Further Reading

Books

Barcella, Laura. *Know Your Rights!: A Modern Kid's Guide to the American Constitution*. New York, NY: Sterling Children's Books, 2018.

Elish, Dan. *The Civil Rights Movement: Then And Now (America: 50 Years of Change)*. Mankato, MN: Capstone Press, 2018.

Roosevelt, Eleanor and Michelle Markel. *When You Grow Up to Vote: How Our Government Works For You*. New York, NY: Roaring Brook Press, 2018.

Websites

The Brennan Center
brennancenter.org
A nonpartisan center that focuses on democracy, especially on voting rights.

Congress For Kids
congressforkids.net
Website with information about elections and the national government, aimed at kids.

The Martin Luther King, Jr. Research and Education Institute at Stanford
kinginstitute.stanford.edu
Contains documents by the famous activist, curriculum, and history of the Civil Rights Movement.

Index